CALGARY FLAMES

BY DAN SCIFO

Copyright © 2023 by Press Room Editions. All rights reserved. No part of this book may be used or reproduced in any manner whatsoever, including internet usage, without written permission from the copyright owner, except in the case of brief quotations embodied in critical articles and reviews.

Book design by Maggie Villaume
Cover design by Maggie Villaume

Photographs ©: Tony Gutierrez/AP Images, cover; Brett Holmes/Icon Sportswire, 4–5, 7, 19; Jeff McIntosh/The Canadian Press/AP Images, 8; Fred Jewell/AP Images, 10–11; Focus On Sport/Getty Images, 13; Ramon Cliff/Shutterstock, 14–15; Al Messerschmidt/AP Images, 16–17; Bruce Bennett Studios/Getty Images, 20; Dustin Bradford/Icon Sportswire, 23; Gary Rothstein/Icon Sportswire, 24–25; Shelly Castellano/Icon Sportswire, 27; Chris Williams/Icon Sportswire, 28

Press Box Books, an imprint of Press Room Editions.

ISBN
978-1-63494-590-5 (library bound)
978-1-63494-608-7 (paperback)
978-1-63494-643-8 (epub)
978-1-63494-626-1 (hosted ebook)

Library of Congress Control Number: 2022912906

Distributed by North Star Editions, Inc.
2297 Waters Drive
Mendota Heights, MN 55120
www.northstareditions.com

Printed in the United States of America
Mankato, MN
012023

ABOUT THE AUTHOR

Dan Scifo lives outside of Pittsburgh, Pennsylvania, with his wife and family. He has covered two Super Bowls, three Stanley Cup Finals, two NHL outdoor games, and two US Open golf championships during a career that spans more than 15 years as a sports journalist. He currently serves as a freelance correspondent for The Associated Press and USA Hockey.

TABLE OF CONTENTS

CHAPTER 1
CALGARY CHAOS
5

CHAPTER 2
MOVING UP NORTH
11

CHAPTER 3
ROAD TO THE CUP
17

SUPERSTAR PROFILE
JAROME IGINLA
22

CHAPTER 4
BURNING BRIGHT
25

QUICK STATS	30
GLOSSARY	31
TO LEARN MORE	32
INDEX	32

1

Matthew Tkachuk tallied six points in the seven-game playoff series against the Dallas Stars in 2022.

CALGARY CHAOS

The Calgary Flames hadn't won a National Hockey League (NHL) playoff series in seven years. One more win could change that.

It was Game 7 of the first round of the 2022 playoffs. The Flames and Dallas Stars were tied 2–2 in overtime. That meant the next goal would win it.

Less than five minutes remained in the first overtime.

Matthew Tkachuk took possession of the puck for Calgary. A Dallas defender pushed him behind the Stars' net. So Tkachuk shoveled a quick pass to Johnny Gaudreau. Stars defenders then smothered him. Gaudreau had to make a quick decision.

Gaudreau passed to Elias Lindholm in front of the net. The forward fired a shot at the Dallas goalie, Jake Oettinger. The shot bounced off Oettinger's mask and kicked back towards Gaudreau.

The Flames were dominating on offense. They had taken 66 shots on goal compared to the Stars' 28. Gaudreau was ready to let rip number 67. He gathered the puck and blasted a shot from the

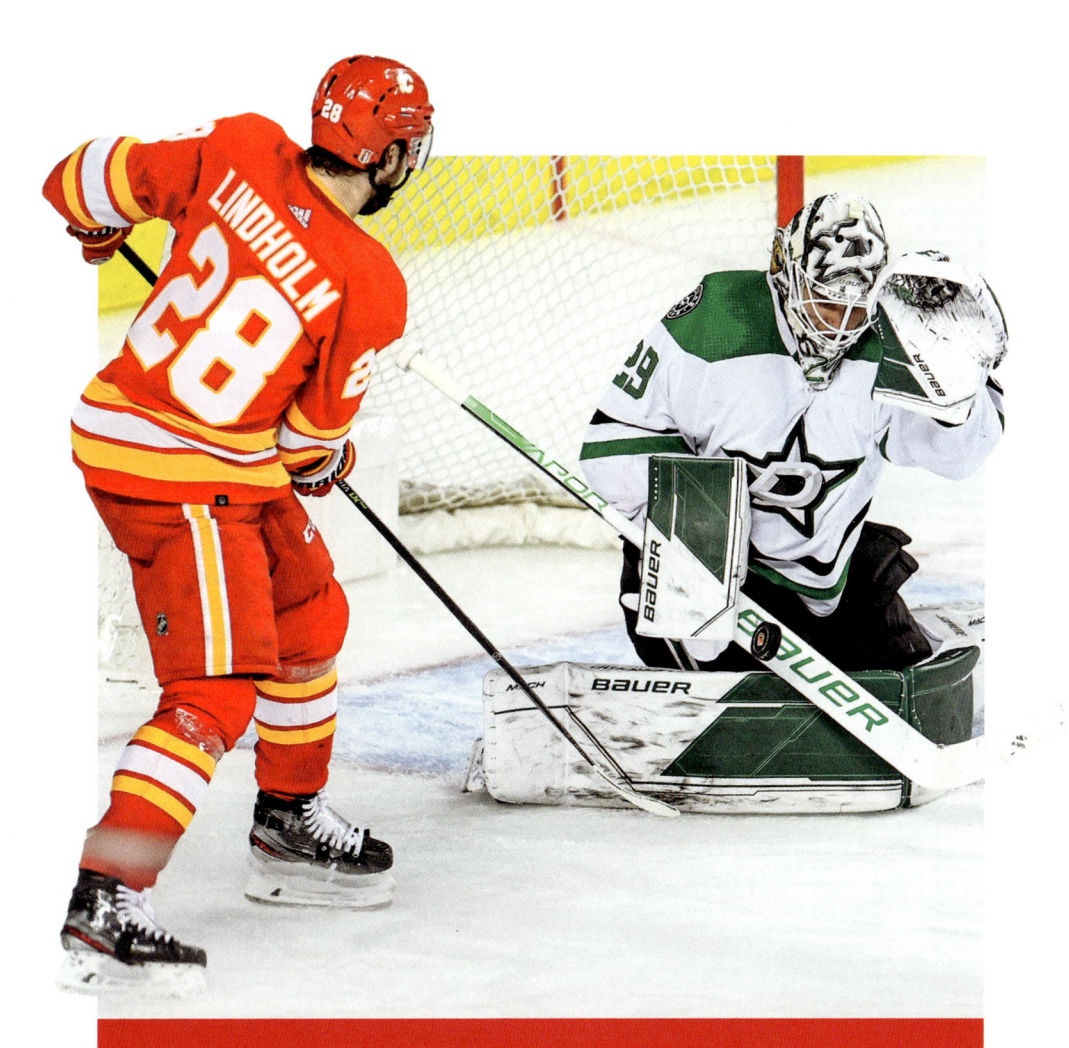

Elias Lindholm has his shot stopped in Game 7 against the Stars in 2022.

left face-off circle. Oettinger was still recovering from the previous save. He got there too late. The puck sneaked past his right shoulder and into the net.

The Flames surround Johnny Gaudreau and celebrate winning the first-round series against the Stars.

Gaudreau threw up his arms in celebration. His teammates mobbed him against the wall. Oettinger could only lower his head in defeat as his teammates came to console him. The roars of the Calgary home crowd were deafening.

The Flames had won 50 games that regular season. Only one Calgary team had ever won more. Now the Flames were off to the second round to continue the run. But they still had work to do. Their biggest rival, the Edmonton Oilers, awaited in the second round.

•HISTORY IN ALBERTA

The Flames started the 2022 second-round series against the Oilers hot. They scored two goals in the opening 51 seconds. That was the fastest two goals for a team to start a playoff game in league history. In Game 5, the teams combined to score four goals in 71 seconds. That was the fastest four-goal stretch in playoff history. However, the Oilers went on to win the series in five games.

2

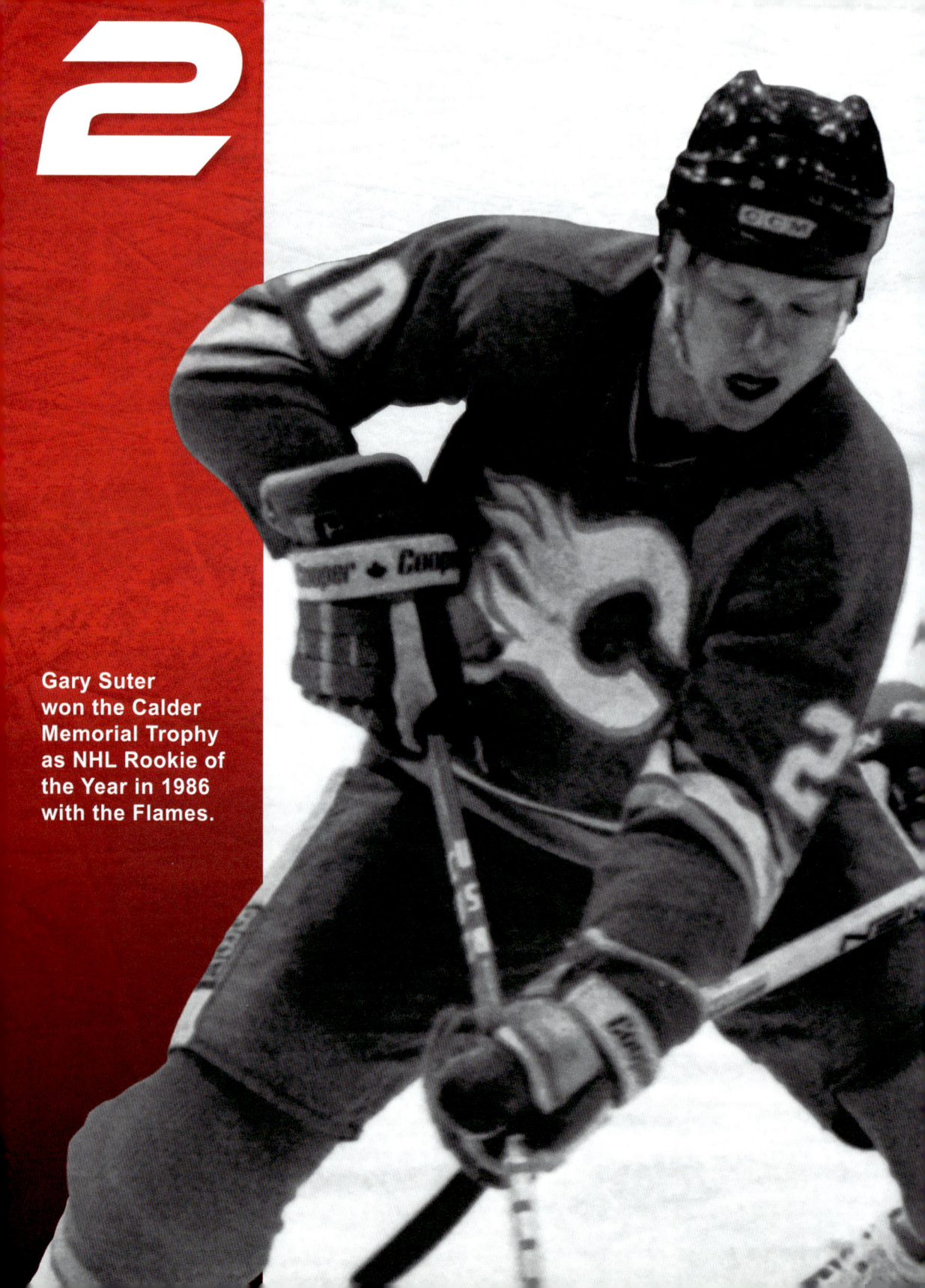

Gary Suter won the Calder Memorial Trophy as NHL Rookie of the Year in 1986 with the Flames.

MOVING UP NORTH

The Flames were founded in 1972. But they didn't play in Calgary. In fact, they didn't even play in Canada. The team played its first eight seasons in Atlanta. The Flames missed the playoffs two of their first three years. Then they reached the postseason the next five years. However, attendance at games was low. By 1980, the Flames decided to find a new home.

In May 1980, the Flames moved to Calgary. Their first game took place on October 9, 1980. A standing-room-only crowd showed up at Calgary's Stampede Corral. They saw the Flames tie the Quebec Nordiques 5–5.

The Flames' first season in Calgary was a special one. They won their first two playoff series. Center Guy Chouinard was at his best during the playoff run. He tallied 17 points in 16 games. But it wasn't enough. Calgary lost in the conference finals against the Minnesota North Stars.

Several stars shined for those early Calgary teams. In 1980–81, center Kent Nilsson set the team record with 131 points. Right winger Lanny McDonald

Kent Nilsson recorded more than 100 points in a season twice with Calgary.

scored 66 goals two years later. That was a team record, too.

Meanwhile, Calgary returned to the playoffs in 1982. The Flames won playoff series each of the following two years. However, both times they lost against Wayne Gretzky and the Edmonton Oilers. The Alberta cities are separated by a three-hour drive. That made them natural rivals. However, the Oilers dominated the Battle of Alberta in the 1980s.

By 1985, the Flames had qualified for the playoffs for a 10th consecutive season.

The Saddledome got its name because the arena's roof is shaped like a horse saddle.

However, they had yet to reach the Stanley Cup Final. Greater success was on the horizon.

HOME AT THE SADDLEDOME

The Flames played their first game in Calgary at the Stampede Corral. But the Saddledome has served as their permanent home since 1983. The Saddledome is one of the oldest arenas in the NHL. It seats close to 20,000 fans. The first game there took place on October 15, 1983. The Oilers picked up a 4–3 win against the Flames.

3

Gary Roberts tallied 505 points in 10 seasons with the Flames from 1986 to 1996.

ROAD TO THE CUP

The Flames finally got past the Edmonton Oilers during the 1986 playoffs. It was the first time they'd beaten their Alberta rivals in the playoffs. Thousands of fans flocked to the streets of downtown Calgary to celebrate. But the Flames weren't done after that. They made their first trip to the Stanley Cup Final. However, that's where the run ended. The Flames lost in five games against the powerful Montreal Canadiens.

Calgary's first 100-point season came in 1987–88. Joe Nieuwendyk helped lead the way. The center scored 51 goals. Only one rookie had previously surpassed 50 goals in a season. Nieuwendyk also won the Calder Memorial Trophy as the NHL's top rookie that year.

The Flames couldn't make it back to the Final, though. They were eliminated by fellow Canadian teams in 1987 and 1988.

The Flames earned a team record 117 points in 1988–89. The playoffs didn't start as planned, though. The Vancouver Canucks nearly upset the Flames in the first round. Calgary goaltender

Banners hang in the Saddledome for Mike Vernon and Al MacInnis. Both played for Calgary for 13 seasons.

Mike Vernon made sure that wouldn't happen. He stopped Vancouver's Stan Smyl on a breakaway in overtime of

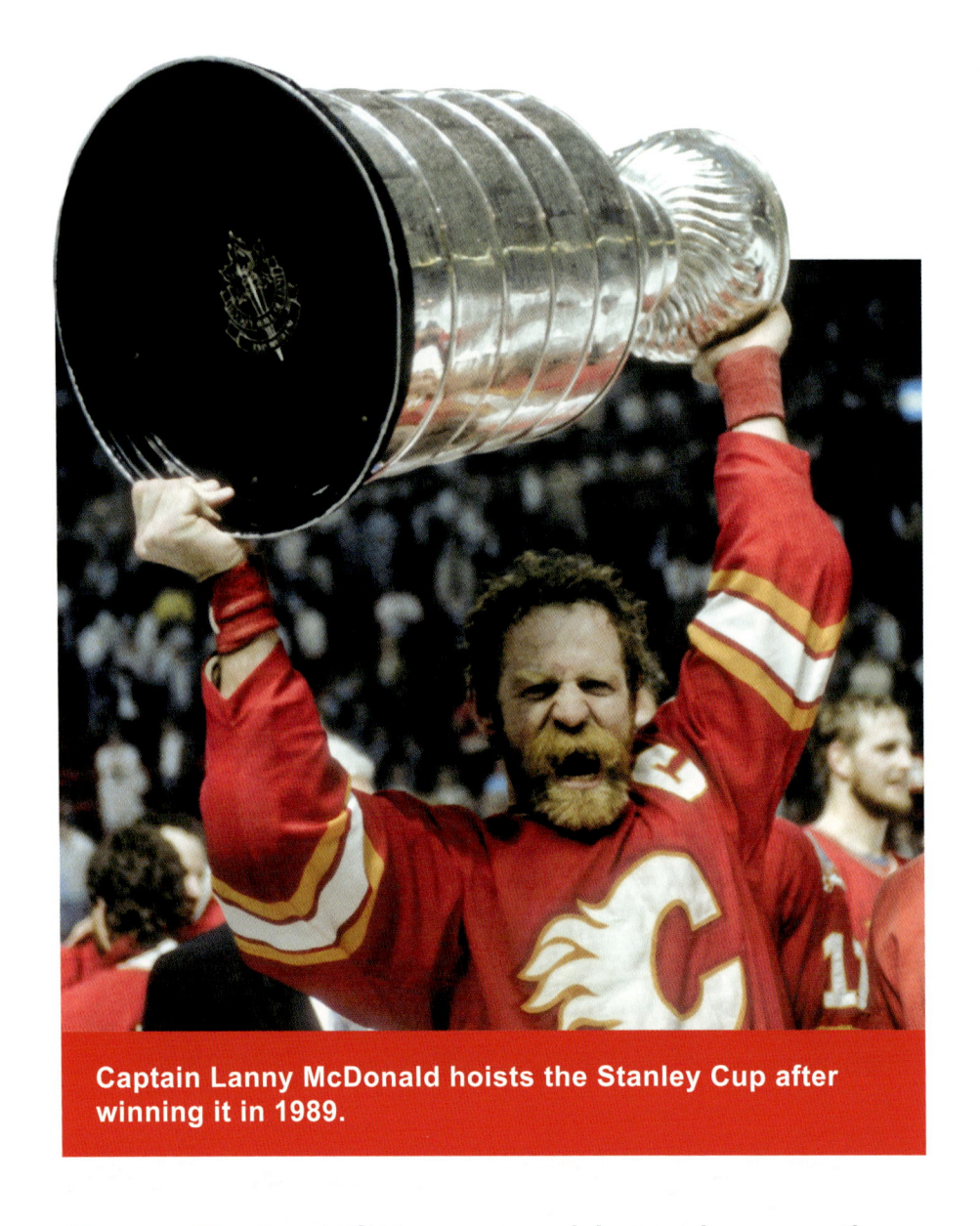

Captain Lanny McDonald hoists the Stanley Cup after winning it in 1989.

Game 7. Joel Otto scored later in overtime to send the Flames on to the next round.

The Flames met a familiar foe in the Stanley Cup Final. It was a rematch with Montreal. This time, Calgary took home the trophy in six games. Lanny McDonald scored a goal in Game 6 to help secure a 4–2 win. It was a special moment for Calgary fans. And it was extra-special for McDonald. He had been to the playoffs 12 times before 1989. But he hadn't won a championship. The 36-year-old retired after lifting the Cup with the Flames.

•ENSHRINED CHAMPIONS

Five Hockey Hall of Famers played on the Flames' Stanley Cup–winning team in 1989. The list includes team captain Lanny McDonald. The other four were Joe Mullen, Al MacInnis, Joe Nieuwendyk, and Doug Gilmour. All four finished among the top five in regular-season scoring for Calgary. The Flames later retired the numbers of McDonald, MacInnis, and Nieuwendyk.

- **SUPERSTAR PROFILE**

JAROME IGINLA

Jarome Iginla made his NHL debut as an 18-year-old in the 1996 playoffs. Then he played 16 more seasons with the Flames. The high-scoring right winger became the face of the team.

Iginla was best known for his goal scoring. He won the Maurice "Rocket" Richard Trophy as the NHL's top goal scorer twice. Those goals meant a lot to Calgary. In the 2000–01 season, Iginla started donating $1,000 per goal to a Calgary charity. He raised more than $500,000 in his career. By 2013, the Flames were rebuilding and traded Iginla. He left having played in 1,219 games for the Flames. He scored 525 goals and collected 1,095 points. All were team records.

Iginla's No. 12 was retired by the Flames in 2019. He was elected to the Hockey Hall of Fame in 2020.

Jarome Iginla's 625 career goals are tied for 16th-most in NHL history.

4

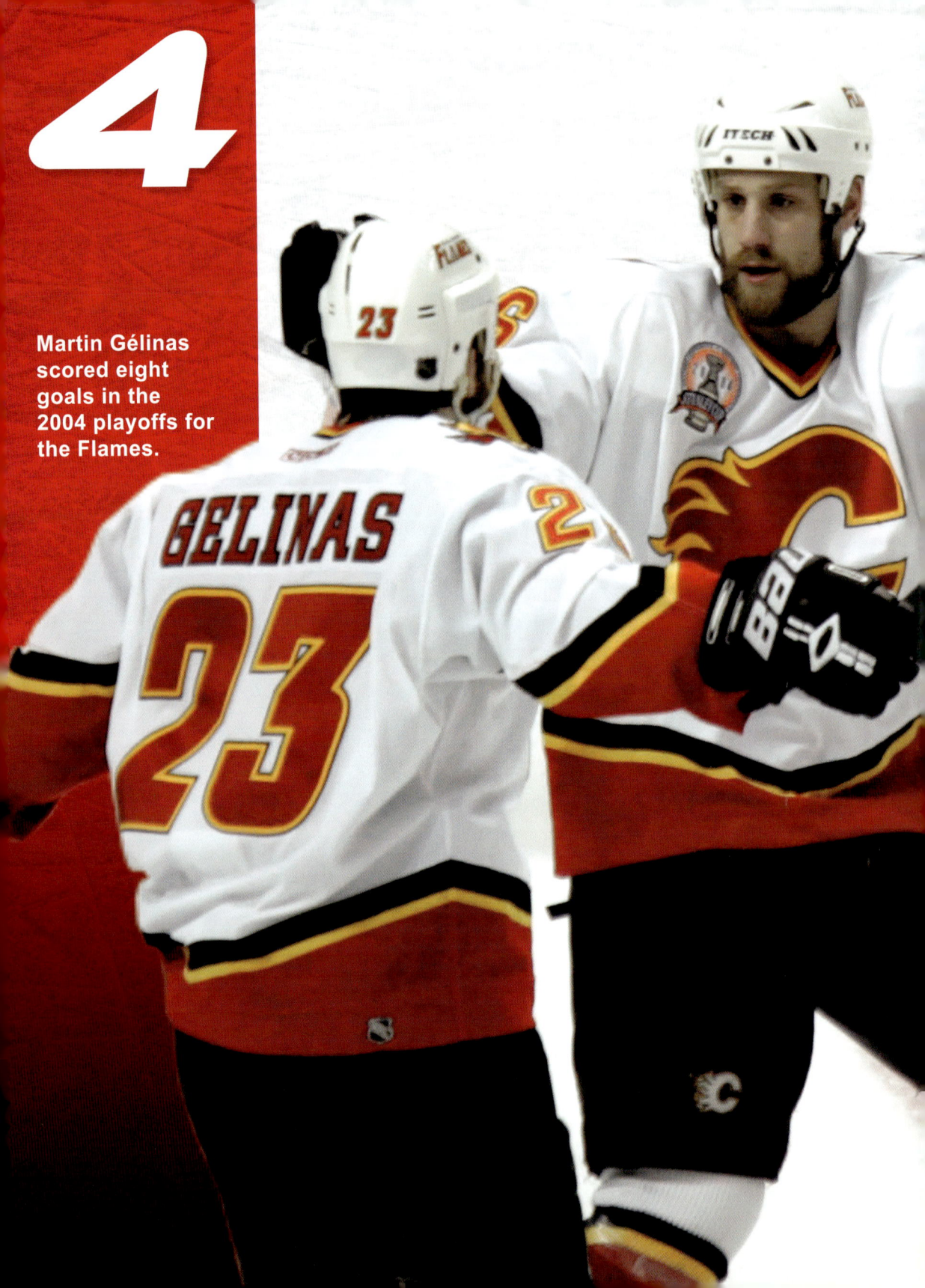

Martin Gélinas scored eight goals in the 2004 playoffs for the Flames.

BURNING BRIGHT

Calgary didn't win another playoff series for a while. It took until 2004. But the Flames won more than just one series. They made a run all the way to the Stanley Cup Final. The Tampa Bay Lightning awaited. Up 3–2 in the series, Calgary had a chance to clinch the championship at home in Game 6.

With the score tied 2–2 late in the third period, controversy stuck.

Flames forward Oleg Saprykin sent the puck on net. It was saved, but the puck then bounced off Martin Gélinas's skate to the front of the net. The Tampa Bay goalie stopped the shot near the goal line. Or did he?

The officials reviewed the play. No replays made it clear if the puck had crossed the goal line. No goal was awarded, and play resumed.

Martin St. Louis ended up scoring a goal in double overtime for the Lightning. Two days later, the Lightning won the Stanley Cup in Tampa.

The Flames were able to bounce back after the disappointment, though. In 2005–06, they had their best regular

Miikka Kiprusoff makes a save against the Los Angeles Kings in a 2004 game.

season since 1988–89. Miikka Kiprusoff was a big reason why. He won the Vezina Trophy as the NHL's best goalie. But the Flames lost in the first round of the playoffs. It would be a while until they won another playoff series.

As a 21-year-old, Johnny Gaudreau tallied nine points in 11 games in the 2015 playoffs.

In 2014, Johnny Gaudreau made his NHL debut. The left winger, nicknamed "Johnny Hockey," helped reignite the Flames. Gaudreau led the Flames to the team's first playoff series win in 11 years. They beat the Vancouver Canucks in six games in 2015. The young star had six points in the series. After eight seasons, he was already among the Flames' top five in points and assists.

But Gaudreau left after the 2021–22 season. Then the Flames traded away Matthew Tkachuk to the Florida Panthers. They got star left winger Jonathan Huberdeau in return. Calgary fans are hopeful players like Elias Lindholm and Huberdeau can keep the Flames contenders for years to come.

GIORDANO LEADS THE WAY

The Flames named defenseman Mark Giordano their captain in the 2013–14 season. He was replacing Jarome Iginla as Calgary's leader. In 2018–19, Giordano won the Norris Trophy as the NHL's top defenseman.

CALGARY FLAMES
QUICK STATS

TEAM HISTORY: Atlanta Flames (1972–80), Calgary Flames (1980–)

STANLEY CUP CHAMPIONSHIPS: 1 (1989)

KEY COACHES:

- Bob Johnson (1982–87): 193 wins, 155 losses, 52 ties

- Terry Crisp (1987–90): 144 wins, 63 losses, 33 ties

- Darryl Sutter (2003–06, 2021–): 172 wins, 109 losses, 15 ties, 26 overtime losses

HOME ARENA: Scotiabank Saddledome (Calgary, AB)

MOST CAREER POINTS: Jarome Iginla (1,095)

MOST CAREER GOALS: Jarome Iginla (525)

MOST CAREER ASSISTS: Al MacInnis (609)

MOST CAREER SHUTOUTS: Miikka Kiprusoff (41)

*Stats are accurate through the 2021–22 season.

GLOSSARY

ASSIST
A pass that results in a goal.

CAPTAIN
A team's leader.

CHARITY
An organization that helps raise money for those in need.

OVERTIME
An additional period of play to decide a game's winner.

RIVAL
An opposing team that brings out the greatest emotion from fans and players.

ROOKIE
A professional athlete in his or her first year of competition.

TO LEARN MORE

BOOKS

Berglund, Bruce. *Big-Time Hockey Records*. North Mankato, MN: Capstone Press, 2022.

Monson, James. *Behind the Scenes Hockey*. Minneapolis, MN: Lerner Publications, 2020.

Nicks, Erin. *Johnny Gaudreau: Hockey Superstar*. Burnsville, MN: Press Box Books, 2019.

WEBSITES

To learn more about the Calgary Flames, go to **pressboxbooks.com/AllAccess**.

These links are routinely monitored and updated to provide the most current information available.

INDEX

Chouinard, Guy, 12

Gaudreau, Johnny, 6, 8, 28–29
Gélinas, Martin, 26
Gilmour, Doug, 21
Giordano, Mark, 29
Gretzky, Wayne, 14

Huberdeau, Jonathan, 29

Iginla, Jarome, 22, 29

Kiprusoff, Miikka, 27

Lindholm, Elias, 6, 29

MacInnis, Al, 21
McDonald, Lanny, 12, 21
Mullen, Joe, 21

Nieuwendyk, Joe, 18, 21
Nilsson, Kent, 12

Oettinger, Jake, 6–8
Otto, Joel, 20

Saprykin, Oleg, 26
Smyl, Stan, 19
St. Louis, Martin, 26

Tkachuck, Matthew, 6, 29

Vernon, Mike, 19